P9-EDT-283

BUTTERFLY
WISH

Also by S. S. Dudley

Elf Hills
Book 1 of the *Elf Hills* series

www.ssdudley.com

Butterfly Wish

written by

S. S. Dudley

illustrated by

Andrea Hartman

Stoddard
BOOKS
Davis, California

For Sofia. May you always believe in fairies. — *S. S. D.*

For my mom, a great art supporter. — *A. H.*

* * *

This is a work of fiction. Names, characters, businesses, places, events and incidents are either the products of the author's imagination or used in a fictitious manner. Any resemblance to actual persons, living or dead, or actual events is purely coincidental.

Text copyright © 2014 by S. S. Dudley
Cover art and illustrations © 2014 by Andrea Hartman.
All rights reserved. Published by Stoddard Books.

This book or any portion thereof may not be reproduced or used in any manner whatsoever without the express written permission of the publisher except for the use of brief quotations in a book review. For information regarding pricing and licensing for use in schools or libraries, write to Stoddard Books, P.O. Box 72773, Davis, CA 95617 USA.

ISBN: 1942609027
ISBN-13: 9781942609025

Visit www.ssdudley.com.

Contents

BUTTERFLY
WISH

Chapter One

BIRTHDAY WISH

Selara Mary Leda was having the best
day ever. At last it was her birthday!
Mom and Dad—who were the best
mom and dad in the whole wide world
—had organized a fabulous birthday
party for her with all of her friends.

Balloons, ribbons, prizes in colorful bags. A butterfly piñata and a butterfly cake with lots of blue frosting. Pinks and purples and yellows and blues everywhere. It was so beautiful. If only her friends would come.

"When are my friends coming?" Selara asked her mom again. She had asked lots of times, but they never came.

"Soon dear, very soon now."

"Okay..." Selara said, pushing a strand of her long, dark hair out of her eyes. She went to sit under her butterfly piñata in the garden.

And then Selara's friends came. Soon she had friends everywhere. They ran. They screamed. They jumped. They laughed.

Selara was on top of the world. It was her day!

Until Johnny Silverton—who was a much smaller 4-year old—decided he would play with Selara's plastic sword. He was a pirate—"Har! Har!"—and he waved the sword and chased the girls.

But this was *Selara's* day and *Selara's* sword. So she, who was much bigger and grown-up, ripped the sword from little Johnny's hands and decided that she would be the fierce pirate. No—a prince. No—a warrior princess!

Selara screamed and laughed and chased her friends.

Little Johnny screamed and cried great sobbing tears.

Selara's mom stopped Selara with a frown and told her to share her toys. "Return that sword to Johnny right now," she said.

Selara refused.

Mom repeated herself.

Selara refused again and turned to walk away.

"If you want cake and presents, Selara Leda, you will give the sword back right now!"

"OK!" Selara yelled, dropping the sword.

"Thank you, dear," said Mom.

Selara stomped off, a big wrinkly frown on her pretty, round face. Mom was no longer the best mom in the whole world. Best-mom wouldn't have taken *her* sword away. But Selara wanted her cake.

After a little while—she played hopscotch very nicely with Margaret and Luisa—Selara sought out her mom again.

"Can we do cake now?" Selara asked, jumping up and down and batting her big, green eyes.

"Okay, call your friends."

"Yes!" Selara shouted. "Time for cake!"

Soon all of Selara Leda's friends were gathered around the large blue, butterfly-shaped cake. Butterflies were Selara's favorite critter. They were *so* beautiful.

The bug-shaped candles were lit. Her friends and family sang "Happy Birthday." It sounded so awful, she couldn't help but giggle. And then it was *that* moment. Selara closed her eyes and made her wish. With a little smile, she took a big breath and blew hard on the dancing flames. It took a couple of tries, but she blew them all out.

"I want vanilla ice cream! Two scoops!" she declared.

Selara Mary Leda was normally a good girl. And she had a very nice fairy godmother who normally kept an eye on her. But on Selara's birthday, her fairy godmother, Misty Meadow, was flying hard. She was eager to see her family, who lived a long way away. Misty had left her magical fairy godmother locket behind for her replacement, another fairy, named Burt Buttles. He was going to be Selara's substitute fairy godmother while Misty was gone, which wasn't supposed to be long.

This was a good thing, because Burt Buttles was not really a fairy godmother. Technically, he was a wood sprite. He didn't have a clue about being a fairy godmother. In fact, Burt was a rather naughty fairy who had gotten in trouble recently for putting brown in a rainbow. Imagine, a rainbow with brown in it! It hadn't even been one of his better stunts. He had just been bored. Of course, a nosy water fairy had seen Burt's rainbow and told on him. Burt's punishment was to serve as a substitute godmother fairy. The other fairies thought this would make Burt act more responsibly. Burt doubted it. They had told him that if he kept Selara safe until Misty returned—only a few days—he would be free again. It sounded easy enough to him. So he had put on Misty's shiny silver locket with Selara's hair inside, tucked it under his shirt, and set off.

It had been easy to find Selara. The locket led him right to her. She was in the middle of a party. Burt wandered around, bored, and settled down near the cake, licking frosting every now and again. When Selara got in trouble for taking a plastic sword from a little boy, Burt had felt a strange tingle in his fingers. It didn't seem right to Burt that Selara should get in trouble. The sword and party were Selara's, after all. Burt began to think of what he could do to help Selara. Isn't that what the fairy godmothers were supposed to do? He didn't really know, but it sure seemed that way to him.

To his surprise, Burt knew what Selara wished for when she blew out her candles. It came to him as an image in his head. His fingers tingled more, making him feel uncomfortable. Then he realized that, as a godmother fairy, he could do magic when Selara needed it. He smiled and laughed, "Ha ha!" Selara needed his help. As soon as she fell asleep, he could grant her wish. It would be fun. This fairy godmother thing might not be so bad after all...

Chapter Two

BUTTERFLY

Selara Leda woke and thought that she felt very warm. She looked around and wondered if she had fallen asleep in the garden, there was so much green. There were plants everywhere!

She stretched and flapped her wings.

Flapped her wings?

Selara looked over her shoulder and gasped in surprise. Her wish had come true, she was a butterfly! With blue wings.

She tried them again. They were real. Could she fly? She flapped harder and let go of the leaf she was standing on. Wow, she was flying! She flew up and did a loop like butterflies do, then she soared up high. She dove, she twirled, she drifted...she giggled uncontrollably. She felt *amazing*.

Then Selara felt tired. Flying was hard work. She landed on a branch and looked around. She didn't know where she was. It was not her backyard, or the park down the street, or any place she knew. Everywhere there were trees and plants and leaves, leaves, leaves. Not even any flowers. Where was this? She listened. Chirps, whirs, a rattle of leaves...

"HELLO! Isn't this incredible? Ha!"

Selara Leda jumped and tumbled and would have fallen on her pretty wings if she hadn't flipped over at the last moment. She looked up.

Before her stood the most curious little man. He must have been very small, because he stood atop a leaf. He also had wings. One looked like it was missing a piece. *Who are you?* Selara thought. She felt shy and didn't know if she could make a sound with her new mouth—butterflies don't make sounds—but the little man understood.

"I am your godmother fairy. Call me Burt," he said with a large smile. Then he put his hands on his hips and looked around.

Selara hesitated. Her fairy god-mother? He didn't look like a fairy! He had a beard, long hair, and was dressed in brown. And he was a *he*.

Burt turned back to face her, still grinning. "Oh, some of us are more like god-daddies or god-uncles, I guess. I granted your wish, do you like it?" he asked.

Selara thought about it. Flying was fun, yes, but she felt a little lonely and lost. She nodded. Then she looked around at all the green.

"This is the Amazon rain forest. Amazing, huh? You wanted to be a big blue butterfly and this is where those live."

Selara thought about what Burt said. Amazon? Rain forest? She knew about that, it rained lots and monkeys lived there.

Finally Selara felt she could speak. "Which way is my house?" she asked. She wanted to show her friends how she could fly.

Burt smiled again. "I don't know! Ha! But here you can play however you want. Come on, let's fly." Burt bent his legs to jump.

Selara felt sad. Here she had neither friends nor toys. "I want to go home," she said.

Burt snorted, hovering just a couple of inches above his leaf. "What? But there is so much fun to have! Come on now, you have wings. Let's fly!"

Burt zipped up into the air. Selara noticed his wings buzzed like a dragonfly, while her big wings made a very soft *whoosh* as she flapped them.

Selara didn't want to be alone, so she followed Burt. They flew up high to where the sun shone bright, zoomed down into the shadows under the trees, and then climbed high again. There were so many trees, and birds and ants... *Ants everywhere!* she thought. But then she tired again and started to feel hot and hungry. She really wanted to go home. A strawberry popsicle would make her feel much better.

Burt finally stopped zipping about. He landed on a very long, wide leaf. Selara landed too. She smelled something sweet and it made her hungrier.

"I'm hungry," Burt said.

Selara wiggled her antennas.

"Come on," he said.

She followed him up the leaf. There was something hanging from the tree: big and bulky with lots of curved, yellow blobs. *Bananas*, Selara realized as Burt opened one and scooped out a handful of fruit. She jumped in near him and poked her long mouth (it was called a proboscis, she remembered) into the banana. It tasted heavenly.

They ate and ate.

"Ah, that's good, huh?" Burt said, wiping his hands on his brown shorts, leaving bits of banana behind.

Selara tried to nod. Her bushy antennas bobbed in front of her eyes.

Burt stretched and burped.

Selara wanted to giggle. But she was beginning to feel sad again.

"Are you really my fairy godmother?" she asked.

Burt scratched his belly. "Well... yes, I am. But only for a little while. Your regular fairy godmother is traveling." He looked around as if searching for someone.

Selara stared at him. She had known it! He couldn't be her real fairy godmother, he was too... hairy. "Where did she go?"

"I don't know, some family thing. She'll be back soon." Burt shifted his shirt and hopped on his toes a couple of times. It looked like he was getting ready to fly again.

"When?" she asked.

"When what?"

"When does she come back? I want to go home—"

Burt abruptly cocked his head as if hearing something. "Oh geez, I need to go. I'll be back later. Bye!"

And before Selara could say or think a thing, Burt buzzed up and away and was gone. She tried to watch where he went, but she saw only leaves, leaves, leaves. It felt really quiet. Something chirped nearby. A bird? A spooky yell echoed in the distance. Another butterfly, smaller and with orange and black in its wings flitted overhead. Selara hoped it would stop to talk to her, but it didn't.

Selara was a big, beautiful, blue butterfly that could fly—for real! Only she had no one to show. She was all alone in the Amazon rain forest, wherever that was, atop a big leaf with nothing but banana to eat. She wanted her mom. She wanted to cry. Except it didn't seem butterflies could cry.

Chapter Three

MONKEY & ANTEATER

BAM!

Selara fluttered up in fright.

"Hello there, Heh-heh-heh, you are a sad, Heh-heh-heh-heh, butterfly," said a gentle, giggly voice from below her.

Selara carefully flew close and saw a cute face stare back at her. It looked like a baby, kind of, with more fur. A monkey! The monkey grabbed a banana and began to eat it, peel and all.

"You're a monkey," Selara said with a happy giggle, forgetting she was a butterfly.

"Heh-heh-heh," chittered the monkey. "You butterfly, heh-heh-heh." He grabbed another banana.

"No I'm not, I'm a girl," Selara said.

"Heh-heh-heh. You butterfly."

"No. A fairy made me a butterfly, I really am a girl."

"Heh-heh-heh. Me too. No fairy made me! Heh-heh-heh." The monkey giggled around a mouthful of banana. He had bad manners, Selara thought.

Selara wasn't sure how to talk to this monkey. He ate another banana.

After a little while he stopped and looked at her.

"You really girl?" he asked.

She nodded.

"You make wish?" he asked.

Girl Selara would have hung her head sheepishly. Butterfly Selara couldn't. "Yeah... but I didn't want to come here! Can you help me get home? I don't know which way it is."

"Where home?"

"Davis, California."

The monkey shook his head. "No know California. Talk to anteater, Heh-heh-heh, she very smart."

Selara frowned. "Where's the anteater?"

"Heh-heh-heh, eating ants!" the monkey giggled and with a rustle of leaves, dropped out of sight.

This must be a dream, Selara thought. She would wake soon and go rushing into her mom and dad's room to tell them all about it. She waited a little. Then she got bored. She tried closing her eyes. But she discovered butter-flies can't close their eyes. Nothing had happened. She was still on the leaf.

With a little butterfly shrug, or shrugs, since she had 4 arms, of course, Selara decided to look for the anteater. What else was she to do?

Now, where to look?

She had seen ants on top of the trees, on the trunks and branches, and on the ground. Everywhere really. *Can anteaters climb?* she asked her-self. Maybe she would start looking among the leaves.

So she did. Selara flitted high and in and around and over tree upon tree after tree after tree. She saw birds, other butterflies, and even some monkeys. No anteaters. Selara tried to remember what an anteater looked like. Was it big? Small? Long nose? Short nose? Shaggy fur? No fur? Hmm...

Selara drifted down through the leaves and began to wander carefully among the branches looking for anything that might be eating ants. *Did anteaters eat butterflies*, she wondered suddenly. Hopefully not. She was too pretty to be eaten. Plus, she was really a girl.

Before long, she heard a scraping sound. Curious, she flew in the direction of the sound. She saw a big, black blob sticking to a tree branch.

The sound was coming from it. *Strange*, she thought, flitting closer. The blob was hard, like dried clay. It was shaking! *This is scary*, she worried. She started to turn around, then she saw it.

Something like a big, hairy squirrel sat in the tree. It was digging at the blob with very long claws, making it shake. As Selara watched, the hairy squirrel stopped digging, stuck its long nose into the hole it had made, and ZIP-ZIP-ZIP out flicked its super long tongue. What was it doing?

She couldn't help herself. She flew closer. There were thousands and thousands of little specks streaming out of the hole. *Ants*, Selara realized. Tiny black ants. *Oh!* This must be the anteater! It was licking up little ants like she licked up Super-Sour Nerds.

"HELLO," Selara cried. She didn't actually make any noise, but the monkey had understood her.

The anteater ignored her with a snort. It licked up some more ants.

"Excuse me, the monkey said I should talk to you."

Another snort.

"Please?"

The anteater turned toward her, finally. It flicked its long, pink tongue. "No, no. No utter-lie today, thank you," the anteater said to herself in a mommy's voice. Ms. Anteater spoke funny.

"But I'm a girl. My fairy godmother turned me into a butterfly," Selara said.

The anteater turned back toward her. "Oh dear, tsk," she said. Then she resumed eating ants.

"He isn't my real fairy god-mother." Selara watched the anteater slurp up more ants. They were crawling all over her now, but she didn't seem to notice. "Do you know where California is? I want to go home."

"Alihornia? Ne-er heard of it, dear," said the anteater.

Selara felt sad. She didn't like being lost. She found a branch to rest on and tried to cry again.

After a little while, the anteater looked up at her.

"Go see the jaguar, dear. He goes all o-er," the anteater said in a gentle voice.

The jaguar? But jaguars are big, fierce cats, Selara thought with fear. The anteater must have understood, because she said "Don't orry. He likes utter-lies, 'ut not to eat!"

Selara smiled a butterfly smile. "Where is he?" she asked.

"Oh, around. Wander down there and try going that way," the anteater pointed with her long, slender nose.

"Okay," said Selara.

"Good luck."

"Thank you." And Selara let herself fall from her branch, gliding toward the ground to search for the jaguar.

Chapter Four

A Bird!

WHOOSH!

Selara did a somersault. "Oh!" she shouted. Something had almost hit her.

She flew up toward a tree and looked around. *There*, it was a bird with a yellow belly and a big sharp beak and it was coming right toward her.

"Wait!" she shouted.

The bird ignored her. Its beak was open. It was going to eat her!

"EEEEKKK," she screamed, diving at the last moment.

WHOOSH!

This time the hungry bird came so close she felt its wings. Being a butterfly was no fun if you were chased. If only she were something bigger...

Selara heard a buzz from somewhere nearby. She felt different—bigger, heavier. She was falling... and then she reached out with a long hand and grabbed a branch, stopping her fall and swinging in the air.

The yellow-breasted bird squawked and veered off into the branches.

"Bad bird!" Selara yelled, hanging from her branch. She looked down. She was no longer a butterfly. She had fur and a long tail and long hands... she was a monkey!

"Sorry!" chirped the bird. "I was chasing a tasty butterfly."

"I'm not a butterfly. I'm a girl!" Selara said.

The bird cocked its head as it pulled its wings out of the leaves. "You are a monkey..."

"I only *look* like a monkey."

The bird was quiet.

"Can you tell me where the jaguar is?" Selara asked.

The bird laughed. "Why do you want to find *him*?"

"The anteater told me he would know the way to California."

"But he'll eat you!" said the bird.

"Silly! Jaguars don't eat butterflies!"

The bird cocked its head again. "But you're a monkey."

Oh. Selara looked down at her furry self. She must look very cute. And tasty to a jaguar... *Oh no, now what?* That bad fairy Burt. Where was he? "Do you know where California is?" Selara asked the bird as it was about to fly away.

The bird looked down at the ground, then up, then left and then right. "That way maybe? Yes, I think that way." And he pointed to his right. *Or was that left?* Selara asked herself. And then he flew away.

Being a monkey was almost as good as a butterfly. There were so many branches and trees in the Amazon forest that she could swing everywhere. And she never fell. She couldn't wait to tell her best friend Isabella. Isabella loved monkeys.

Selara swung along happily. *Wow*, she would rule the monkey bars back home!

What was that?

Something had moved below her. She peered through the leaves. But she was swinging between branches and forgot to look where she was going. She missed a branch!

"Auugghhh!" Selara screamed as she fell...

Then she felt a tug on her butt and she stopped falling. She was swinging upside down. Looking up, she saw that her tail was wrapped around a branch. Selara giggled. Her tail! She could swing with her tail too!

Again something moved below her. Was it the wind? No. Some animal was on the ground. It moved again. It was big. And brown.

Selara craned her neck, still swinging.

A big, long head appeared and looked up at her.

"EEEK!" squeaked Selara.

"UUUH-UUUH," grunted the weird animal below. It had dark, beady eyes and a long nose. It looked almost like a pig, but bigger.

The animal watched her for a moment, then began sniffing around the ground. It pulled up a small tree and started to chew it.

Selara giggled.

The animal looked up again and grunted.

"What are *you*?" Selara asked, swinging down lower.

The strange animal said nothing. It chewed and chewed. Selara slipped closer, using her tail and arms to climb down the tree. She liked having a strong tail. Why didn't people have tails?

CRASH!

Selara squeaked and zipped back up the tree. Another of the animals had appeared, and another. These looked at her and then started pulling up bushes and branches to munch on. Selara stared at their long noses. They could move them around, like a finger... or an elephant's trunk! She loved elephants!

"Are you elephants?" Selara asked. Maybe their noses hadn't grown yet. Hmm...their ears seemed too small.

"UUUH-UUUH," said the animal.

Selara pouted. Why wouldn't it talk to her? All the other animals talked to her. Maybe they couldn't hear her. She swung down low again. The animal was so big! She could nearly touch the back of the first one... Selara reached out a long brown monkey arm...

"Teh-teh-teh-teh-teh-teh..." chittered something loudly.

Huh?

Selara stopped and looked up. There, nearby, was a squirrel. A real squirrel, sitting on another branch and watching her. *That's weird*, Selara thought. A squirrel in the jungle? It flicked its bushy tail.

BUZZZZ.

Selara waved a hand at a big bug flying near her ear.

"Hey! Watch it!" said a familiar voice.

Selara stopped waving. There, hovering nearby, was her bearded fairy.

"I wouldn't make the tapir mad," Burt said.

"What?" Selara asked.

"Tapir!" Burt pointed at the big animal below.

"Oh!" said Selara. Tapir, that was its name? Or was that what it was? Like she was a monkey, er, a girl...

"They're the biggest animal you'll find here," Burt said, admiring the animals.

Selara looked at Burt and back at the big animal below her. It was big. Big enough for girl Selara to ride, definitely big enough for monkey Selara. She hesitated. Part of her wanted to make Burt take her home. But a bigger part was having too much fun as a monkey. *Just a little while longer*, she thought.

"Mr. Tapir, can I touch you?" she asked the tapir.

The squirrel chittered and climbed up higher.

"UUUH!" grunted the animal, thrashing its head.

Oh no, it was getting mad. Why?

"I think he's a she," Burt whispered behind his hand.

"Oh! *Miss* Tapir, can I touch you?"

This time the tapir grunted softer and kept eating. So did the others.

Selara reached out and touched Miss Tapir's big back. The hair was stiff and pokey.

"Do you know the way to California?" she asked Miss Tapir.

Miss Tapir snorted.

Burt laughed. When Selara turned to scowl at him though, he had disappeared.

Selara decided Miss Tapir's snort meant she did know the way. So Selara jumped on the tapir's big back. Now she would get home soon. She didn't need Burt. And when she got home, her friends would be so amazed to see her as a monkey riding a weird elephant-pig. Selara couldn't wait to go to the park and show off her monkey acrobatics. It was going to be *so* fun!

Chapter Five

KING JAGUAR

Selara was bored. The tapirs were slow. And all they wanted to do was eat, eat, eat!

"Are we there yet?" Selara asked.

Miss Tapir grunted. Again.

"Ugh. This is so boring!" Selara whined.

A branch hung low and close to Selara. She grabbed it and stuffed a leaf in her mouth to chew on. Weird, she thought monkeys ate fruit, but the leaves were tasty. A big, fat caterpillar sat on one of the leaves. She looked at it. It looked at her. It was green and fuzzy. She was hungry... her mouth watered... she brought it close to her mouth... *BUMP!*

Miss Tapir jumped down from a root, startling Selara.

"Auck! Gross!" Selara wailed, throwing the leaf and caterpillar away from her. *Monkeys ate bugs too? Weird.*

Miss Tapir stopped walking and lifted her big head. She turned it, listening.

"What? What is it?" Selara asked, excited.

"UUUH! UUUH! UUUH!"

Selara sighed. Tapirs were worse than baby brothers: impossible to understand. Miss Tapir suddenly started to run, surprising Selara, who tumbled off and onto the ground.

"Wait!" Selara called, jumping to her feet—and tail. The tapirs were all running. She watched them disappear into the trees and bushes. Quickly, she climbed the closest tree and started swinging through the branches. It was easy to follow them, they were so noisy. She swung through the trees effortlessly, her strong hands, feet, and tail always finding a branch or vine to grab. It was almost as good as flying. *This is fun!*

Then she heard a big splash. And two more. *Water?*

Selara swung faster. All of a sudden there were no more branches in front of her! Oh no! She tried to turn back, but it was too late.

"Auugghhh!" she yelled and fell, straight down.

SPLASH!

Can monkeys swim?

Selara paddled to the surface. She floated. Monkeys *can* swim! And there were her tapir friends, standing in the middle of what looked like a pond, staring at her. She smiled.

"Hi! This is fun," Selara said to them. She decided they had wanted to cool off in the water. It was hot in the jungle.

"UUUH," grunted Miss Tapir.

"Uuuh," grunted another, smaller tapir. Selara imagined this was Miss Tapir's daughter.

Selara turned back around and started to swim to shore. The water felt good, but as a monkey it was more fun to swing. Maybe Burt would turn her into a fish next.

"YEEEOWWRRR!"

Selara froze. She looked up into big yellow eyes. Big yellow eyes and big, white, sharp teeth! What was this?

"YEEOWWRRR!" it roared at her.

It closed its mouth and watched. Selara watched back. It was a kitty cat. A very, super, ginormous kitty cat with spots. Oh, this must be the jaguar!

Selara was very excited for a moment, then she remembered she was a tasty monkey. The jaguar licked its lips. It started to enter the water.

"No! Stop! I'm not a monkey! I'm a girl! I'm trying to go to California! The anteater said you knew where it was!" She began paddling toward the tapirs as fast as she could. Only... the tapirs were gone. *What? Where were they?*

There was a splash behind her. The jaguar was going to catch her! Where was Burt? If she were a fish she could swim away.

She saw the jaguar jump toward her. She squeaked. There was a buzz and a tingle and suddenly all she could see were bubbles. She was under water! She was a fish. No, she had legs. Then the jaguar's huge paw appeared next to her. Selara kicked her feet hard...

... But nothing happened. She wasn't going anywhere! She tried again, kicking harder. And then the water dropped away from her. She felt squeezed. It was hard to breathe.

"Ow!" Selara whimpered.

The jaguar grunted and relaxed its strong jaws.

Selara took a big breath. She looked down at her short, thick, green legs with scales... what was she now? She could still feel that she was in the air, being lifted by the jaguar, but she couldn't feel its teeth. And if she pulled her head back, it felt like she had a roof. A turtle! She was a turtle! She would be safe now.

The jaguar carried Selara the turtle back to the bank and set her down. She pulled in her head and legs and tail and peeked out at the big kitty. He

was as big as the tiger at the zoo. The jaguar lay down in front of her, licking his massive paws.

"I eat turtle, you know," he said with a rumbly voice that made Selara shiver.

Oh no, Selara thought. He was going to eat her! "Please don't eat me Mr. Jaguar, I'm really a girl..."

The jaguar grunted and swatted at her with a big paw.

"Auck!" she screamed.

But it was a very gentle pat. The jaguar smiled a kitty smile.

"Miss Anteater told me about a girl with a naughty fairy who wants to go home to Alornia," he rumbled.

Selara peeked out again from her shell. "California, please."

"Ah! Califorrrrrrrrrnia," he purred. "Well, then, what shall we do to get to California?"

"You know where it is?" Selara asked, growing bolder.

The jaguar grunted. "I am KING of this jungle, I know where everything is."

Selara thought about that. "But isn't the lion…"

"YEEOWWRRR!" roared the jaguar.

Selara ducked back into her shell and would have squeaked if she had been a girl.

The jaguar laughed. "There are no lions here little girl! Here jaguars are kings!" And he roared again, but this time it didn't scare Selara.

"Now, little one, where is this naughty fairy?" the jaguar asked.

Selara shook her small turtle head. "I don't know. I wished to be a butterfly, and he made me into one, but brought me here. And now whenever something bad is about to happen he changes me to something else and goes away. But I just want to go home." Selara felt sad and would have cried a little, but, like butterflies, it didn't seem turtles could cry. So she pulled her head back into her shell. Having a shell was like carrying a playhouse on one's back. It was so cozy and safe inside. One of her favorite books was about a turtle.

"I see," said the big cat. He sniffed the air and turned his head left and right. "Well, I think CALIFORNIA is that way. Shall we?"

And before Selara could answer, King Jaguar took her in his mouth—

gently—and began to walk through the forest.

Chapter Six

THE LADY

"Where are we?" Selara asked. King Jaguar set turtle-Selara down on some mud. Water splashed behind her. She stuck her feet out, lifted off the ground, and slooooowwwwly turned around. This was not the pond they had just left. This was a beach. Water stretched on for forever!

"I will call it 'califorrrrrrnia'," the jaguar said, with a rumbling laugh.

"California?" Selara said. It looked like the ocean, but there were no waves. And there were still endless trees around her. "Where are the people?"

"Wait," said the king, lying in the shade of a big tree and yawning a big yawn full of long, pointy teeth.

Selara waited.

Selara began to feel cold. That was weird, wasn't it supposed to be hot in the jungle? A patch of sunlight was in front of her. She crawled to it slowly. Ahhh! So warm!

The jaguar looked her way. Afraid, Selara tucked into her shell. What if the jaguar was waiting to eat her later? Maybe she could swim away. Turtles were good swimmers. Could she get home by swimming? Being a turtle wasn't as interesting as a butterfly or a monkey, but she had a shell to protect her and her friends would still be amazed.

She heard a big snort. King Jaguar lay on his back, his feet in the air, eyes closed. His belly was covered with fuzzy white fur. Selara would have loved to touch that fur, it looked so soft. But what was that sound? Then he made it again. "AAAHRRR-FOOO." He was snoring!

This was it, her chance to get away. Selara planted her stubby feet and began to walk toward the water. Oh, she was so slow! After having been a butterfly and a monkey, being a turtle was terrible. She finally understood the story about the rabbit and the turtle, but couldn't believe a turtle would ever actually win any race. Her shell made it so she could only inch forward, one step, two steps, three, four, five–so close to the water, only a couple more... and then the ground was gone.

Huh?

She was floating in the air. But she was still a turtle! She could see her stubby turtle feet with their long claws and if she pulled her head back, there was her shell above her head. What was happening? Turtles can't float in air!

"Tah-tah," clucked a voice. The world spun. *Oh no*, now what had her? She closed her eyes and pulled her head, legs, and tail deep inside her shell.

"Tah-tah, who you?" said a chirpy voice.

Selara dared to open one eye. When she saw an old lady looking at her, her other eye popped open too. And her head popped out from the shell, she was so surprised.

"Hee-hee-hee," laughed the old lady. She seemed nice, with a big smile wrinkling her very wrinkly, brown face.

"YEEOWWRRR!"

Oh no, the jaguar! What would he do to the nice lady?

"Shush!" said the lady, waving a hand. She looked back at Selara and winked one eye. "Silly kitty."

"Yeeowrrr," said the jaguar again, in a much softer voice.

"Who you?" the wrinkly lady asked again.

"Selara Leda," Selara said, not sure the lady would understand turtle.

"Woo hoo! Pretty name. Selara. You come." And the lady started to walk, carrying Selara.

They went a short way to a small house. Out front was a big cooking pot.

"Woo hoo! My house Selara Leda. You like?"

Selara stuck her head out and looked around. It was a very small house tucked under a big tree. *A tree house*, she thought. "I love it!"

"Woo hoo! Maybe I put you on my wall." And the lady held turtle-Selara up against the wall. With a gulp, Selara noticed several other turtle-like shells hanging there.

What is the wild old lady doing? thought Selara.

"Woo hoo! First you go in my soup."

And with that, the lady dropped Selara into her cooking pot. She was going to be made into turtle soup!

It was no use. Selara couldn't get out of the black pot. The sides were too slippery. The little brown lady was doing something, but all Selara could see were leaves and a little bit of sky above her. Where was her fairy godmother?

PLUNK!

Selara saw the lady's hands. She was dropping something into the pot. Pieces of white something. Potatoes?

"Don't eat me! I'm a girl!"

But the little old lady ignored her and hummed a song as she dropped more potatoes.

Selara closed her eyes and tucked back into her shell, like hiding under the covers of her bed. *This has to be a dream. Wake up, Selara!*

The lady left. Selara heard rustling sounds. Then she saw a wisp of smoke. Smoke! Oh no! "Help!" Selara shouted as loud as she could.

Selara heard a buzz. She stretched out her neck and looked up. Burt hovered above the pot, his eyes wide.

"Help!" Selara said.

Burt pointed.

Two hands appeared, clapping over Burt. "No you don't! Gotcha!" she heard the lady say. Burt disappeared.

Selara was still a turtle, she could see her shell above her head. The water was getting hotter and now Burt was caught! What was she going to do?

The lady's smiling face appeared in the opening of the pot above her. She reached a wrinkly, brown hand in and lifted Selara the turtle up high. Selara tucked her head, toes, and tail into her shell as far as she could.

"Tah-tah," said the lady, a little smile on her face. She carried Selara toward her house.

"Tah-tah, looky here," said the lady.

Look where? Selara tried to look around, but she was afraid to stick her head out. She could see the little wood house, the jaguar lying down, the short wrinkly brown lady... and a cage of some sort with a butterfly in it. No, a dragonfly. No! A fairy! *Her* fairy!

"Let me out of here!" Burt shouted.

Selara stared. Fairies could be caught?

"Nya-nya," said the little lady, waving her finger at Burt. "Naughty naughty."

Burt buzzed furiously.

"Use your magic!" Selara yelled at him.

Burt's face turned red he was so mad.

"Nya-nya. Godmother fairy only use magic to help child," the little old lady said, putting her hands on her hips.

Burt buzzed again and shook the little cage. Nothing happened. He couldn't get out.

The little lady set Selara down by the cage. She popped her legs out and *ran*.

But turtles are *so* slow. The little lady picked her up again. "Nya-nya," she said. "I no cook you. Tell me what you want."

Selara peeked out at the brown, wrinkly face and saw a nice smile there. She suddenly felt shy. Her head slipped out from her shell a little. "Um, I want to go home," she said.

"Where?" chirped the lady.

"California... do you know how to get there?" Selara asked. Something about the lady gave her hope.

"Tah-tah! No, no, no." The little lady laughed and shook her head.

Was she ever going to go home? Selara wondered, again wanting to cry.

"He know!" the lady said suddenly, pointing at Burt.

Burt glared back.

"No he doesn't," Selara said. "He isn't even a real fairy godmother!"

Burt crossed his arms and sniffed. "This is ridiculous," he grumbled.

The little lady looked surprised. She leaned in close to the cage. "He has locket!" she howled.

"Augh! Not so loud. I'm substituting," Burt complained.

"Nya-nya!" the little lady said, turning to Selara. "You make wish, you go home."

Selara looked at her, confused. Then she realized what the little lady meant. Of course! Selara had wished to be a butterfly first, that was why she was in the jungle. So she had to wish to go home... *hmm.* Her mom didn't like turtles or crawly things. But her dad did! He would love to see her like this. Selara tipped her head, deciding whether it would be fun to go home as a turtle or if she would just get stepped on. That would hurt, she was sure, despite her shell.

"You *wish* go home," repeated the little old lady.

Selara looked at her, hesitant. "Uh, okay," she said, turning toward Burt.

He was still scowling, his little arms crossed. He looked too mean to be a fairy godmother. Selara sighed, feeling a little sad. She wanted to go home, but really she wanted to be a butterfly again *and* go home. Flying was so fun.

Maybe she could wish to go home and to be a butterfly again? Perking up at this thought, Selara said slowly to her fairy: "I wish to go home."

Chapter Seven

WISHING...

Nothing happened.

Selara hovered in the old lady's hand. Burt still wasn't looking at her.

"But I made a wish!" Selara protested.

"Let me go!" Burt yelled.

"Tah-tah! Bad fairy!" tsk-tsked the lady. "Call wood fairies!" She turned away from him.

"NO!" Burt's small voice called. Selara looked back. Burt was sticking his small head through the bars of the wood cage. "No, don't call them. I can be good. Just let me out. I'll wish her home. I promise."

The old lady looked at the little fairy, her face becoming so wrinkly Selara couldn't find her mouth or eyes. There was only a little bump where her nose should have been.

"You stay here," said the lady, setting Selara on the ground. From down here the little lady looked super tall, a giant! Then the lady moved to the cage and started to open it.

"YEEOOWWWRRR."

Selara shivered. The jaguar roared so loud! Then he appeared, walking slowly toward them. He was so big!

The little lady looked up at King Jaguar.

"I don't trust him. He is going to fly away," said the king.

"Tah-tah," muttered the little lady, nodding. "Naughty fairy..." She stepped away from the cage as the jaguar approached to sniff it. Burt tried to hide in the corner.

Selara felt something strange, as if a train were passing nearby. She looked around, confused, and then realized it was coming from the jaguar! He was growling!

"I've never eaten fairy," rumbled the jaguar.

"AHHHH! Don't eat me! I taste terrible and I'll make you sick," threatened

Burt.

"I call wood fairies," said the little old lady.

"NO!" yelled Burt.

"YEEOOWWWRRR," roared the king.

"Okay, okay! I was just having fun! I wanted to see the Amazon, you know, meet a nice wood fairy..."

The king showed his teeth. Lots of long, white, *sharp* teeth.

"AHHH! Your breath smells terrible! You have to let me out. And she has to wish for the right thing. I can't do anything, you know. There are rules." Burt smiled and shrugged.

"Hmph," grunted the little lady. She looked thoughtful.

Selara was confused. What was a wood fairy? Why couldn't Burt do anything? Wasn't he magical?

Selara felt herself rise into the air as the little lady picked her up. Then they were eye to eye.

"Why you no want to be girl?" asked the wrinkly face.

Selara stared back. She could stare really good as a turtle, she realized. She never had to blink! What had the little lady asked? Not be a girl? "Uh, I got mad... and I wanted to fly. Girls can't fly! So I wished to be a butterfly."

"See?" Burt said.

"Butterfly live here. Girl live in California," said the little lady.

"Huh?" Selara said.

"You wish be girl. Be Selara."

Selara thought about this. She had wanted to show her friends that she was a butterfly, then a monkey. Now a turtle. It would be fun to go to school as a turtle...

"I am king of this jungle. Not California," said the jaguar, sitting back on his haunches and flicking his long tail.

Selara now stared at him. What were they saying? "You mean I should wish to be me again?"

The little lady giggled happily.

"But..." But Selara didn't want to be Selara. Selara was boring. She wanted to fly and swing...

"Why do you want to go to California?" asked the jaguar.

"Because I miss my friends and my mom and dad. And I want to show them..." She stopped, she was about to say "show them she could fly" but then remembered she was a hard little turtle.

"Tah-tah. Turtle live in forest," shrugged the little lady.

"Jaguars eat turtles, remember. Small, but tasty," rumbled the jaguar, showing her his teeth.

Selara shivered. She didn't like it when something tried to eat her. The bird had scared her. She thought some more, her head bobbing in the air as she hung from the lady's hands.

"Okay..." Selara sighed.

"Make wish, then we release bug," said the lady.

"Hey! I'm a fairy!" Burt hollered.

King Jaguar growled at him.

"I wish to be Selara Leda!" she said, thinking about how strong and pretty jaguars were.

The lady opened the cage. Burt zipped out. A flash of light...

Chapter Eight

THE AMAZON

Burt was gone. Selara looked around. She could see really, really well. Had there been ants on that tree trunk before? And, wow, there were so many smells! Where had they come from?

The little old lady smelled like old leather...

Little old lady? Ants?

She heard a grunt next to her. She looked... right into the jaguar's big face. He was shaking his head.

Oh no! She was still in the forest. Burt had tricked them!

"Bad fairy!" Selara shouted. It sounded strangely like a growl.

The little lady was tsk-tsking. "You make bad wish!"

What? thought Selara. "I wished to be me!"

"Maybe with your words," the jaguar said.

What? Selara felt confused. She looked down at herself.

Uh-oh.

She was covered with fur! Spots! She had big feet with claws! She was a jaguar.

Selara hung her head. Her tummy growled. Why couldn't she go home *and* be a fun animal? A jaguar would impress everyone! She felt sad. And hungry.

Her tummy rumbled again. What did jaguars eat? A big beetle crawled between her fuzzy paws. She contemplated it, licking her lips.

"Don't," said the jaguar, watching her, his tail flicking and bouncing like the tail of a kitty cat that didn't want to be petted any more.

"What? I wasn't going to eat it!" Selara replied with a snarl. Even though she *had* wondered what the beetle would taste like...

"Why you no want be girl?" the little lady asked, her hands on her hips and her face scrunched up in an ugly scowl.

The jaguar grunted, his big yellow eyes glaring at her. "There are enough jaguars in this jungle," he rumbled.

"I do!" Selara said. She flicked her long spotted tail.

They stared at her, expressions unchanging.

"I really do... I just, well, I thought, you know... well, being a girl is boring, and, um, well, I have to start school soon and, well, I don't want to go... oh! It would be so fun to go to school as a jaguar! Maybe we can, um, find California without my fairy?" Selara avoided their eyes. A butterfly appeared and she swatted at it gently, wondering what it would taste like. She was really hungry now.

King Jaguar and the little wrinkly lady shared a look. Selara noticed and wondered what they were thinking. Her parents did that too sometimes. The little lady smiled and nodded.

"What? What is it? We can go to California?" Selara asked.

"Of course you can," the little lady said with a wink.

Why did she wink? Selara wondered.

"What?" growled the jaguar.

"Yes, yes. That way. Looonnng walk. Jaguar take you." The little lady gestured to her left, away from the water.

The jaguar's long tail twitched. "You go on, small one," he said. "I will come in a moment."

Selara looked at him, then at the lady, who smiled and waved. Selara's tummy rumbled again. Sighing to herself, Selara walked away trying to hear what the jaguar and lady were saying to each other. But they spoke too softly. A moment later a large shadow descended on her. She jumped.

"Ha ha," chuckled the jaguar. "You must stay alert in the jungle."

Selara stared at him. *How could he move so quietly?* she wondered, following him into the trees.

"It's hot," Selara whined.

"I'm hungry," Selara groaned.

"My feet are tired," Selara complained.

"Are we there *yet*?" Selara implored.

"I want my mom!" Selara cried.

"Can we stop?" Selara beseeched.

"WAAA!" Selara wailed.

The big jaguar turned to face her. He snorted through his black nose, his breath tickling her long whiskers. "SHHH," he said. "Jaguars are *quiet.*"

Selara ducked her head and whimpered. The big jaguar turned away and continued to push through the dark jungle. Selara followed, careful to jump over a line of big, black ants.

They had been walking for*ever*. Selara thought so, anyway. And they still hadn't eaten anything. She was a little worried about eating, though, because jaguars ate other animals and, well, she liked her food cooked mostly. Her mom had given her raw fish once. Sooshee she called it. Yuck! But the big jaguar walked and walked. How come he never got hungry?

"Can't we hunt something? Or do something fun?" Selara asked. She saw a bird on the ground nearby. She jumped at it, amazed by how fast and strong she was. Not fast enough, though. The bird flitted away with an angry chirp.

"Hunt? Perhaps. What would you like to eat? How about a nice baby deer?" the big jaguar said, sitting and licking a paw.

"Baby deer! Eek, no! I don't know, maybe some fruit or something?" Selara shook her head to stop thinking about eating a baby deer. That would be horrible! But her tummy rumbled anyway.

The big jaguar grunted and rubbed his head with his paw. "Jaguars don't eat fruit, little one."

"Maybe this once? We could pretend it was an animal?"

He laughed and lay down, rolling onto his back and writhing on the ground.

Selara lay down and put her head on her paws. A mosquito buzzed in her ear. She flicked her tail at it. Another mosquito buzzed in her other ear. She flicked at it. Another mosquito...

"AUGH!" she wailed, jumping to her feet and snapping at the mosquitoes with her mouth. They zipped away and came right back. She swatted at them. More came.

She ran to a tree and started to climb. Perhaps she could get away from the mosquitoes up high. Her claws were strong and she flew up the tree. *Whoa,* she would love to show her cousin Billy how she could climb now.

She stopped on a branch, panting and looking down. The big jaguar looked small from so high. Selara smiled. No mosquitoes!

Then something stung her paw.

"OW!" she yelped.

Something stung her other paw. Then again. And again.

"AUGH!" Selara wailed, dancing on the branch and almost falling. There were little black ants everywhere! They were biting her and it hurt.

So Selara raced down the tree, not nearly so nicely as she had climbed it. She bumped her head and almost fell twice.

When she got back down the big jaguar was rolling in the dirt again, making a strange sound. He was laughing. Selara shook herself and growled.

Selara Leda did *not* like the Amazon jungle.

Chapter Nine

SEARCHING FOR BURT

Selara refused to move. Her feet hurt. Her belly hurt. Her head hurt. Her tail hurt. Everything hurt.

"You don't want to go to California?" the big jaguar asked.

Selara ignored him. All around them were tall trees. Green bushes. Leaves, leaves, leaves. It was dark. There were ants and mosquitoes and spiders everywhere. This was definitely NOT California and they weren't getting any closer. It was going to take *years* and *years* to get there and she was too tired.

A mosquito bit her on the nose.

Selara discovered then that jaguars can cry.

The big jaguar sat, curling his long tail up and around his body to lick at it. He waited patiently for Selara to stop crying.

Selara sniffled and rubbed her face into the ground. "I want to go home."

The jaguar purred. It sounded like a motorcycle.

Selara looked at him. "What do we do?" she asked.

"We find your naughty fairy," he rumbled, standing.

"But how?" Selara sighed. "He is a fairy and can fly and do magic..."

The jaguar snorted. "You are a jaguar now! Jaguars rule this jungle; we can find anything. You just have to know your prey."

Selara felt an ember of hope. He was right, she was a jaguar. She climbed to her feet and shook herself.

"Good," said the big jaguar. "Now, what does your fairy like?"

Selara paused. "Bananas?"

The jaguar laughed. "Fine. Fruit. And I bet he likes wood fairies and a bit of adventure, otherwise he wouldn't be here."

Selara nodded in agreement. That sounded right to her.

The big jaguar sniffed the air and flicked his tail. Selara copied him. She smelled... everything. Flowers and dirt and ants and... she couldn't make out all the things that she smelled. It was overwhelming. How did real jaguars make sense of it?

Fortunately for Selara she was with a real jaguar. And not just any jaguar.

He started to walk off to their right. Selara hesitated slightly before following him. Her paws still ached and she was really hungry. Hopefully they would find Burt fast and she could go home. A big bowl of macaroni and cheese would make her feel so much better.

***

Burt wiggled again. It was no use. He was stuck. He craned his neck and looked around. Still nothing.

"Help!" he shouted.

There was no answer.

Burt trembled.

Chasing a bee—yum, honey—he had run smack into a big spider web. Normally this wouldn't matter, Burt was big enough to break out of most spider webs. But this one was super strong. And he was really tangled up. His head, both arms, a leg and a wing were all stuck to the sticky spider silk. He knew better than to struggle too much. That would just attract the spider, and whatever spider had made this web was a big, dangerous spider.

"Help!" he tried again. But fairies have very small voices.

Burt heard something above him. He squinted into the sunlight. All he could see was a shadow moving his way. Carefully, he twisted his head to move out of the sun. Ah, a bird! With a long sharp beak. Why was it looking so intently at him? It fluttered to a closer branch. He saw it much more clearly now as it turned its head toward him and chirped.

Oh no... Burt thought, shivering suddenly. The bird looked hungry and it was looking straight at *him*. Burt didn't like birds. A bird had taken the piece out of his wing.

Everything was trying to eat him in this crazy place! He closed his eyes and took a deep breath. With as much volume as he could manage he yelled again. "HELP!"

Chapter Ten

THE RESCUE

"There... did you hear it?"

The big jaguar looked at Selara, and cocked his head. A small, faint voice drifted to them from somewhere above. "Helllllllp..."

"Baby bird?" he shrugged.

Selara hesitated. The voice had sounded familiar. What should she do? If she had been her human self she might have chewed her lip. As a jaguar she found that twitching her tail felt better. A little growl also felt good.

Then she heard another faint yelp and made up her mind. She raced toward the voice, but when she heard it again it was behind her. Confused, she stopped. She turned and looked everywhere, but nothing stood out to her sharp jaguar eyes.

"Look UP," said the big jaguar who suddenly appeared next to her.

Selara jumped and squeaked. How did he do that? And he was so big!

She looked up. There was movement in one of the trees. Looking closer, she saw a brown bird perched on a branch and pecking at something. "Hellllllllp!" drifted down, louder this time.

Something about that voice...

The big jaguar looked up, too. "That voice..." he rumbled. "I think that is your fairy."

"What do we do?" Selara asked.

"Those branches are too small for me," he said, his tail twitching quickly.

Selara slumped. If something happened to Burt, what would happen to her? She didn't want to stay a jaguar forever!

"But you should be able to go up there," the big jaguar continued.

Selara was about to reply that she couldn't climb trees very well. Funny how quickly she forgot that she was no longer a girl. She looked up again and chose a tree in front of her. With a leap she began to climb.

It was easy. Again she smiled a big kitty smile. Being a jaguar was fun... sometimes. But no, now she very much wanted to be her again. And to go home. She climbed as fast as she could, which was quite fast actually, and in a moment her head poked through the leaves where she had seen the bird. With a surprised squawk, the brown bird fluttered away into the sky.

Selara watched it go for just a moment before turning her attention to something small that dangled from a big spider web. It was moving weakly and looked like a dragonfly.

"Burt?" she asked.

"Uuuhhhgggg..." grunted the shape.

Selara started to move closer, but found that the branches were too small even for her. They bent under her feet and she realized how high up she was with a shiver. The big jaguar was a very small kitty far down below. Scared, Selara realized she couldn't reach Burt.

"Burt?" she asked again.

There was no response this time. Then Selara saw something move. It was smaller than Burt, brown, kind of fuzzy, and had a lot of legs. *Oh no!* A spider, she realized. And it was moving toward the fairy.

Selara did the only thing that felt right. She growled.

The spider paused, but only for a moment.

Selara looked all around desperately. Below the web were other branches of the tree, bigger branches. She had watched squirrels jump between trees... could jaguars? The spider had almost reached Burt. She knew what would happen if it got to him.

There wasn't any time to think more. Selara jumped as hard as she could, opening her mouth wide to grab Burt.

Selara crashed through spider web, leaves, and branches, wrapping her sharp teeth gently around the little fairy. A branch poked her in the belly. She grunted, but didn't open her mouth. She scrambled to grab onto a branch, something, and then she started to fall. She closed her eyes and thought of her home, her birthday party, her friends, her toys, her clothes. The wind rushed through her whiskers as she fell. Her paw caught

on a branch and she twisted in the air. Her bed... she missed her bed. The little bundle in her mouth squirmed. There was a bright flash of light. Suddenly she wasn't falling. She smelled clean sheets... and then all was dark.

Chapter Eleven

BACK HOME

Selara Leda woke slowly. She had
been having a strange dream. A lady
in a blue dress with a white blanket
around her shoulders was crouched
next to a rock. The lady looked very
sad, and her eyes kept darting to the

sky above. It seemed to Selara that she knew the lady, but she didn't know why. She wanted to find her and tell her that everything would be okay...

Selara rolled onto her side and pulled the blanket up over her shoulder. It was light out. Her mom would come soon, but she was sleepy still. Suddenly she sat up straight and looked around. She was back in her own room! The jungle, the jaguar, it was all gone. Had it all been a dream? It had felt so *real*. She remembered the feeling of having a tail and how natural it had been to twitch it before... before jumping out to grab a fairy from a spider web? She shook her head, but was comforted by the familiar surroundings of her bedroom. There was her baby doll and her favorite stuffed penguin on the floor where they had fallen from the bed. Her closet door had been left open, displaying her play dresses. The blue Cinderella dress was her favorite. And on the walls were her butterflies. Lots and lots of colorful wooden and cloth butterflies. Yes, it must have all been a dream.

She lay back, closed her eyes and rolled over, stretching, wondering who the lady in blue was.

"Auugghhh... I hate spiders," said a small voice from somewhere nearby.

Selara sat straight up, her eyes wide. Had she imagined it?

"Mornin'," said the voice again.

It took a moment for her brain to register what she was seeing. One of her toys was talking to her? It smiled as it stood, but then grunted in pain.

"You didn't have to squeeze me so hard, you know."

And then Selara realized her marvelous dream had not been a dream at all. She was speechless. And then she was angry.

"You're a bad fairy!" she said, flinging a finger at Burt.

Burt frowned and shrugged. "I know, I know. Sorry." He hung his head.

Selara gave him her best glare, scrunching up her nose and eyebrows. But she felt bad when he shrank away. He had answered *her* wish, after all.

"When does my regular fairy come back?" Selara asked. Again she thought of the lady in blue, the one in her dream.

Burt stretched. "Anytime now, I expect." He looked around and frowned. "We shouldn't be talking, you know, I'll get in trouble."

"Harumph. You were already bad."

"Yes, yes. Thanks for saving me."

Selara softened her scowl. "You're welcome."

Burt looked at her and smiled a crooked smile. Then he winked. In a flash he zipped up in the air and flew toward the window.

There was a loud *POP!*

A pudgy fairy in red, yellow curls hanging around his face, his wings beating frantically fast behind him, appeared in the room. Selara's jaw dropped.

"Not so fast Mr. Burt Buttles," said the new fairy in a very high pitched voice, even though this fairy was also a boy fairy.

"Wha—" Burt grunted, hovering by the window.

"Something has come up. Ms. Misty Meadows is delayed. You will continue to watch over... over... um I have it here, what is the girl's name—"

"Selara!" Selara said.

The pudgy fairy did a back flip in the air he was so surprised. "What is this! Speaking to a fairy—er a human! That's against the rules! You'll be in trouble for this, Mr. Burt Buttles!"

Burt hung his head and sighed. "I knew it," he grumbled.

"Now, what was I saying? Oh yes, you must continue to watch over little Selara here. And mind you don't talk to her anymore! Haven't you read the rulebook for fairy godmothers?"

Burt mumbled something.

"Sheesh. Well, you will be advised once we track Ms. Misty down. Keep little Selara safe," the pudgy fairy said. And then, with another *POP!*, he disappeared.

"Ugh," Burt grunted, still hovering by the window.

Selara wasn't sure how she felt about Burt still being her fairy god-mother. Maybe he would do a better job now.

"Selara? Selara? Time to get up dear, it's your first day of school!" Her mom's voice drifted in from outside her room.

Selara stared at Burt. He looked up and waved at her to go, shaking his head.

"Selara!"

"I'm coming!" she replied, climbing out of bed. As she did, something poked her hand. Curious, she pulled back the blankets and found a small branch with a few big, stiff leaves attached. And something fuzzy. She picked it up and looked closer. It was fur. A small piece of yellow fur.

"Selara Leda get up right—" the door suddenly opened and Selara's mom appeared, her eyebrows scrunched. "Oh, come on then. Get dressed. We'll be late."

"OK, mom," Selara said sweetly, her eyes darting to where Burt had been. He wasn't there. She didn't see him anywhere. Her tummy growled. "Mom, can I have eggs, toast, fruit, *and* cereal for breakfast?"

Her mom looked back. "Well some-one is hungry. Running in your sleep again?"

Selara smiled, thinking of the branch safely hidden beneath her bed. "No, flying!"

Dear Reader:

Yeah! You finished *Butterfly Wish*. Thank you. I really hope you liked it. Want more? The **next Selara Leda & Burt Adventure, Wish Upon a Star, is coming soon!**

Would you like to see pictures of the animals in this book? To learn more about them? Maybe see pictures drawn by other readers—including my daughter, Sofia?

To get all of this and find out when *Wish Upon a Star* is coming out, ask a grown-up to **go to my web-site: www.ssdudley.com.** I have a free, fun newsletter your grown-up can get.

Finally, if you enjoyed this book, please consider asking your grown-up leave a review wherever they purchase books. Thanks for your support!

Until next time,

S. S. Dudley

Author's Note

I wrote the first draft of this story in a hotel room not a half-mile away from the Amazon River in Peru. I wrote it for my daughter as a fun way to share my experiences in that magical place (the Amazon—not the hotel!).

Now that the book is done and published, I must first thank my wife for her support, patience, and feedback during the process of producing this (and traveling to Peru). She was the first one to suggest that writing books might be worth doing. I thank my parents, family, and friends for their encouragement. Andrea Hartman provided her beautiful artwork and helped with the book's design. Jamie

Gifford kindly edited the text and provided useful, enthusiastic feedback.

Finally, I thank my kids for the inspiration to write silly fairy tales.

S. S. Dudley
Davis, California
October 2014

About the Author

S. S. Dudley grew up in Cheyenne, Wyoming, in the USA. He spent a lot of time chasing snakes and reading books, back then. He went to school for a very long time in Wyoming and Illinois (some say he was avoiding "real life"). He finally emerged as a doctor of ecology (that's the study of nature) and went off to do science at a big university. He has caught birds in the rain forest in Panama, fish in Antarctica, tortoises in his computer (like a computer game he made up), and mosquitoes in the Amazon and done a whole lot of other "science-y" stuff. He now writes stories when he isn't hanging out with his family or running around his home town in Northern California. Come visit him on the internet at www.ssdudley.com.

About the Illustrator

Andrea Hartman has been drawing and painting for as long as she can remember. She received her BFA from the University of Massachusetts. *Butterfly Wish* is her first illustrated book. She lives with her family in central California, but will always be a Bucks County, Pennsylvania native.

CPSIA information can be obtained
at www.ICGtesting.com
Printed in the USA
FSOW01n1004290115
4841FS

9 781942 609025